THE ALPHABET WITCH

THE ALPHABET WITCH

BY IRENE SMALLS

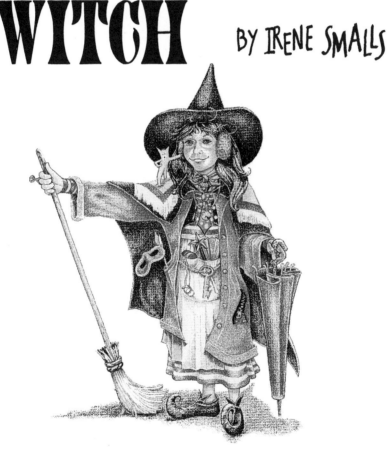

ILLUSTRATED BY KEVIN McGOVERN

Longmeadow Press

To my cousin Cheryl Harris
who taught me the alphabet
I. S.

To Jane and Phineas
K. M.

Published by Longmeadow Press, 201 High Ridge Road, Stamford,
CT 06904. All rights reserved. No part of this book may be
reproduced or utilized in any form or by any means,
electronic or mechanical, including photocopying, recording
or by any information storage and retrieval system, without
permission in writing from the Publisher.
Longmeadow Press and the colophon are registered trademarks.

Cover and interior design by Hannah Lerner

Library of Congress Cataloging-in-Publication Data

Smalls, Irene.
The alphabet witch / by Irene Smalls. — 1st ed.
p. cm.
Summary: Getting ready for bed by taking off clothing named from A
to Z is time consuming for the sleepy witch Xerxes Zainy.
ISBN 0-681-00542-4
[1. Witches—Fiction. 2. Alphabet. 3. Stories in rhyme.]
I. Title.
PZ8.3.S636A1 1994
[E]—dc20   94-6196
CIP
AC

Printed in Mexico

First Longmeadow Press Edition

0 9 8 7 6 5 4 3 2 1

There was a witch named Xerxes Zainy,
Who wasn't very brainy.
Xerxes Zainy used to fret
She could upset the alphabet!

Once when she was sleepy—
So sleepy she was weepy—
She wanted to go to bed
And got mixed up instead.

Do you know what she did?

She took off her **A** part,
Which was her apron.
Her apron she put with her crayon.

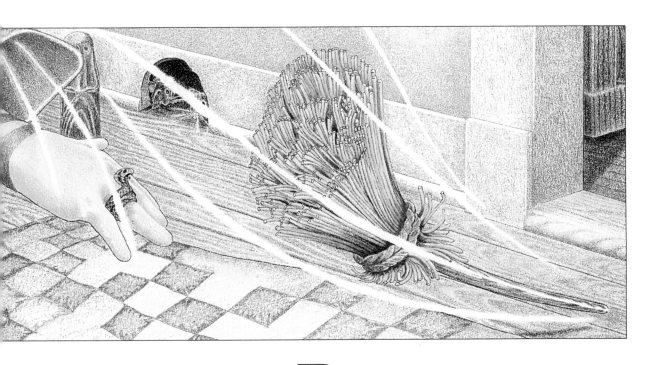

She took off her **B** part,
Which was her broom.
Her broom she threw in the room.

She took off her **C** part,
Which was her cape.
Her cape she hung with tape.

She took off her **D** part,
Which was her dress.
Her dress she left in a mess.

She took off her **E** part,
Which were her earmuffs.
Her earmuffs she put with other stuff.

She took off her **F** part,
Which was her fan.
Her fan she buried in the sand.

She took off her **G** part,
Which was her glove.
Her glove she placed on her dove.

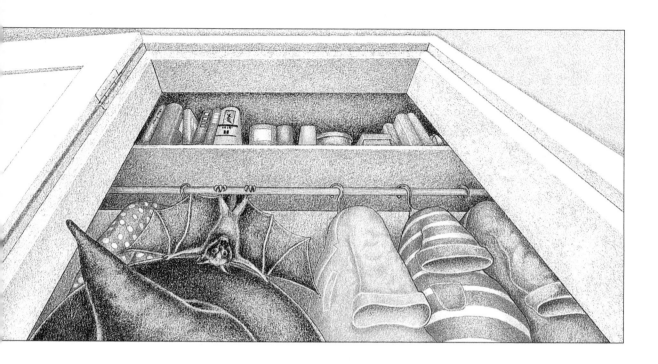

She took off her **H** part,
Which was her hat.
Her hat she put with her bat.

She took off her **I** part,
Which was her It.
Her It she threw in a pit.

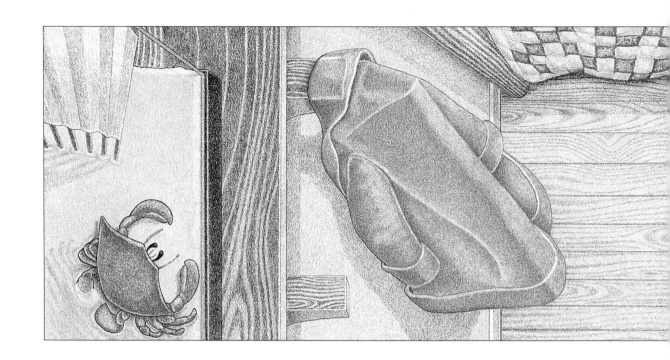

She took off her **J** part,
Which was her jacket.
Her jacket she hung on a bracket.

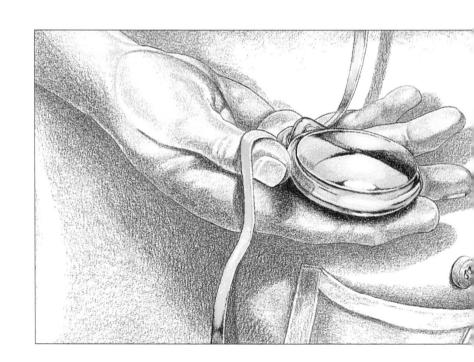

She took off her **K** part,
Which was her key.
Her key she put under the sea.

She took off her **L** part,
Which was her locket.
Her locket she put in a pocket.

She took off her M part,
Which was her mask.
Her mask she put in a cask.

She took off her **N** part,
Which was a neckerchief.
Taking that off was a big relief.

She took off her **O** part,
Which was her ooze.
Her ooze she put down for a snooze.

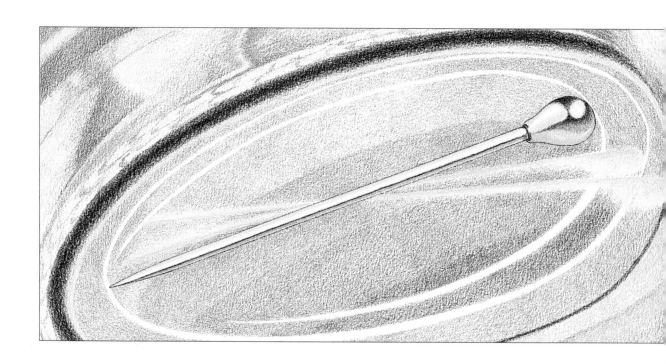

She took off her **P** part,
Which was her pin.
Her pin she set on a spin.

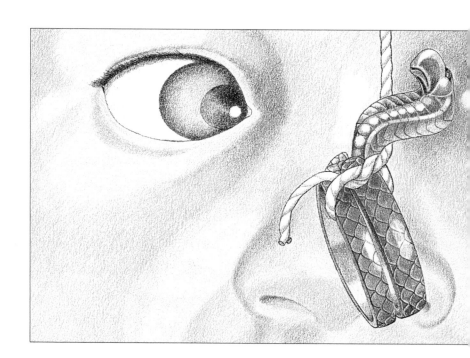

She took off her **Q** part,
Which was her quilt.
Her quilt she put on a stilt.

She took off her **R** part,
Which was her ring.
Her ring she hung on a string.

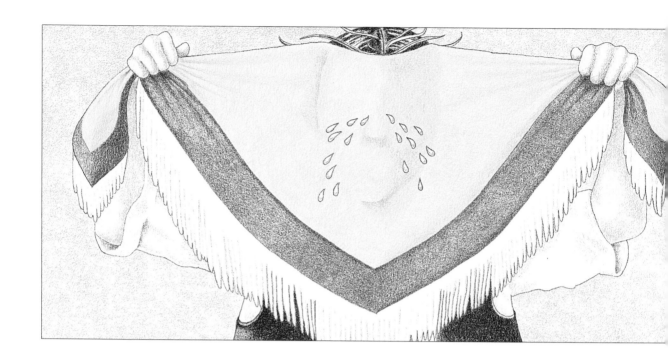

She took off her **S** part,
Which was her shawl.
Her shawl started to bawl.

She took off her **T** part,
Which was her tie.
Her tie she put in a pie.

She took off her **U** part,
Which was her umbrella.
Her umbrella she put in the cellar.

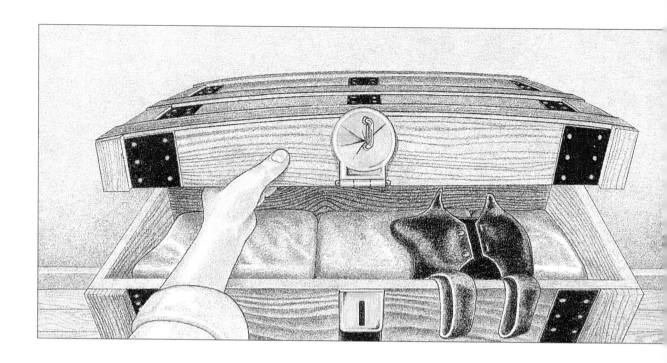

She took off her **V** part,
Which was her vest.
Her vest she put in a chest.

She took off her **W** part,
Which was her wand.
Her wand she threw in the pond.

She took off her **X** part,
Which was Xerxes, her name.
Her name will never be the same.

She took off her **Y** part,
Which was her yo-yo.
Her yo-yo she tied in a bow.

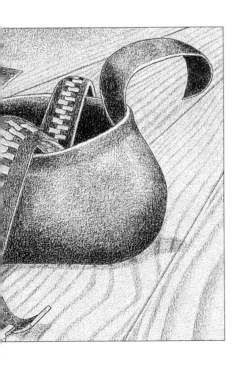

She took off her **Z** part,
Which was a zipper.
Her zipper she put in her slipper.

And by the time she did all that,

Do you know what happened?

It was time to get up!